for Toby

LITTLE TIGER PRESS
1 The Coda Centre, 189 Munster Road, London SW6 6AW
www.littletiger.co.uk

First published in Great Britain 2005
This edition published 2016

A CIP catalogue record for this book is available from
the British Library

 • 978-1-84869-664-8

Printed in China • LTP/1800/1764/1216

2 4 6 8 10 9 7 5 3 1

This Little Tiger book belongs to:

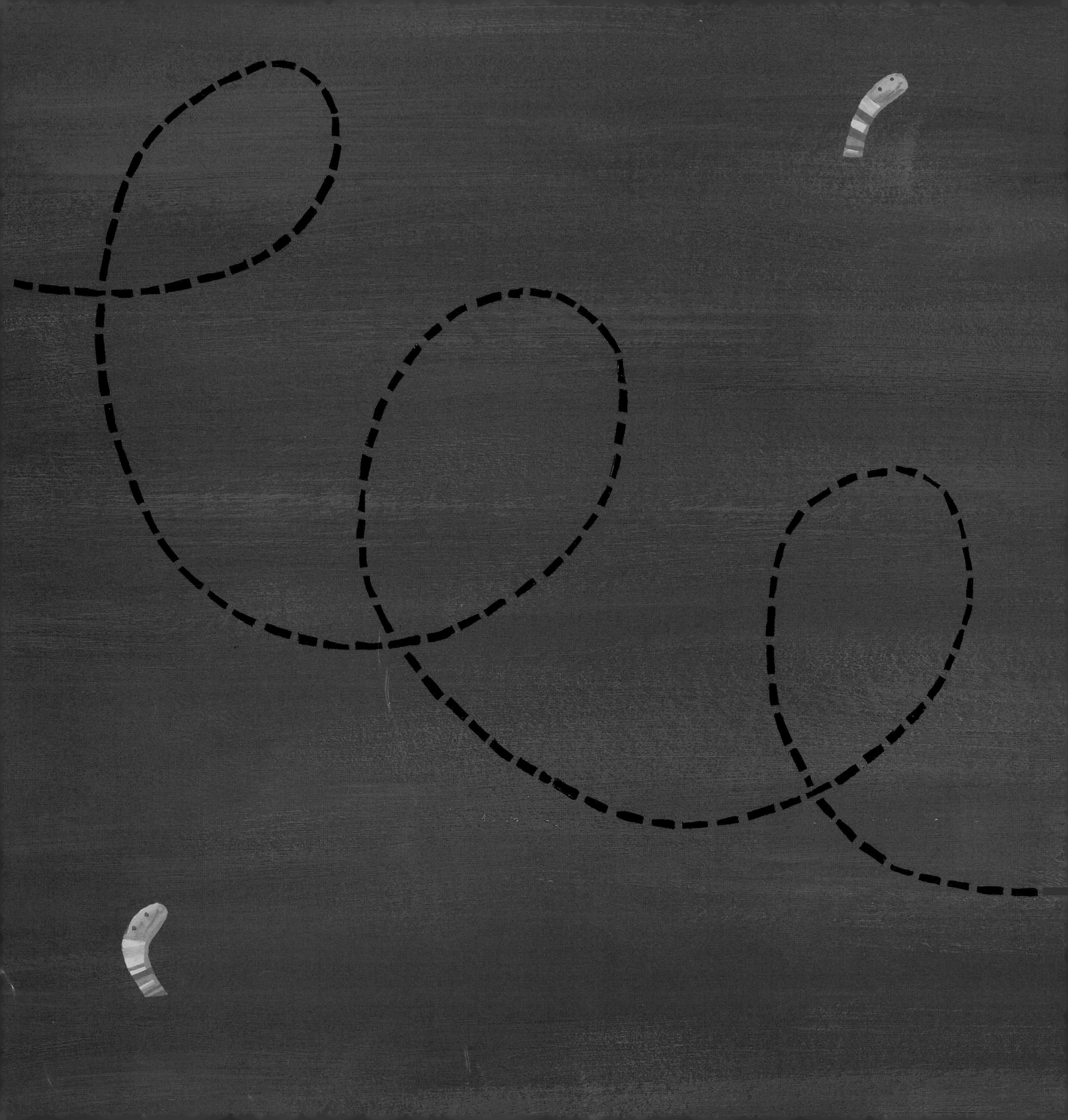

Hoppity Skip Little Chick

Jo Brown

LITTLE TIGER PRESS
London

Little Chick bounced out of
bed one bright sunny morning.
"Let's play, Mum!"
he chirped.

"I need to keep these eggs
safe and warm just a little while
longer, Little Chick," said Mum,
"but I'm sure you'll find someone
to play with in the farmyard."

Little Chick tottered
outside and looked around.
Just then some geese rushed past.
"Honk honk! Follow us!"
they cried.

whiz

ZZZZZZ!

Little Chick thought
that running looked fun.
So he ran too!

Little Chick tootled along –
quite fast for a little chick.

whoOoosh!

Faster and faster he ran, so fast his little chick
legs got tangled up and he tripped . . .

. . . and skidded
into a lamb!
"Meeerrrr!" said
the lamb. "That
looks like fun, but
why don't you
try this?"

And she bounced around.

boing! merrrr! merrrrr!

Little Chick thought that bouncing looked fun. So he bounced too!

BOING! Little Chick managed a little bounce. Well, quite a big bounce for a little chick.

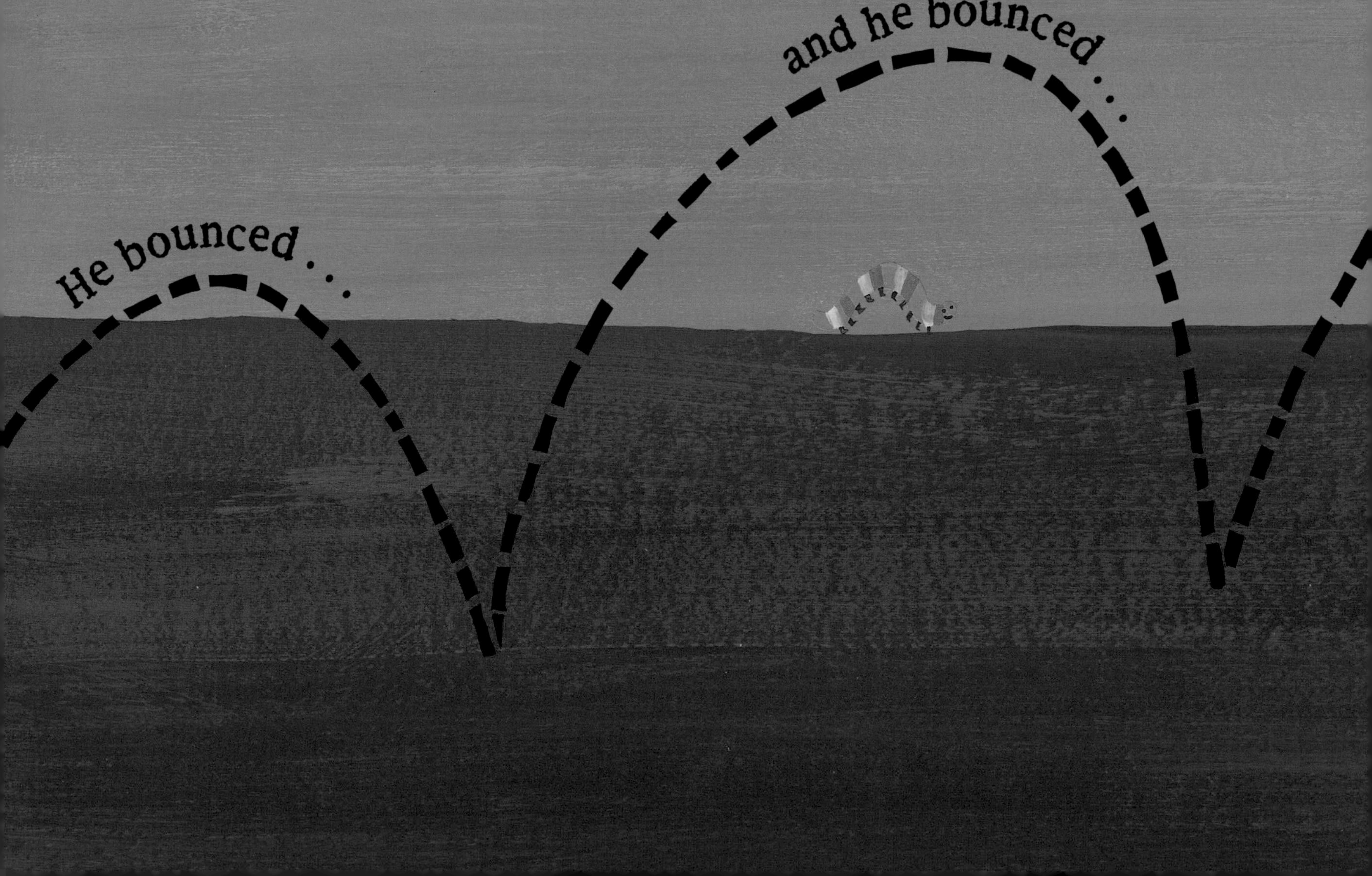

He bounced . . .

and he bounced . . .

and he bounced.
He bounced so high that he whizzed through the air . . .

peeyungggg!

. . . right into a pony!

"Oops!" said the pony. "Nice bouncing, Little Chick, now why don't you jump over this fence with me?"

And the pony jumped
straight over the fence.

Yeee-haa!

Little Chick thought
that jumping looked fun.
So he jumped too!

Little Chick did a little jump . . .
then he did a bigger jump.

Then he did a REALLY
BIG jump, right over the
fence into the next field . . .

Splonggg!

. . . and landed right
on top of a piglet!

"Oops, sorry!" said Little Chick. "I need more practice landing, but jumping is great fun!"

Kersplatt!

"If you think that's fun, try this. It's luuuverly!" said the piglet, and he rolled around in the mud.

"What fun!"
thought Little Chick.
So he scritched and
he scratched . . .

and then he had
a little bit of a roll . . .

and then he did a wiggly
dusty chick dance until there
was dust everywhere.

aaaaachooo!

"This is the best
fun of all!" he cried.

“Great rolling, Little Chick!” said the piglet.

“I’m having so much fun today!” said Little Chick.
“All this bouncy-jumpy-roly-running!
I can’t wait to tell my mum.
See you later, Piggy!”

And he rushed
across the farmyard
to the hen house . . .

. . . where he had a HUGE surprise!

"Hello, Little Chick," said Mum. "Here are your new brothers and sisters."

"Yippee-aye-aayyy!" yelled Little Chick. "Now we can all play together!"

And they played bouncy-jumpy-
roly-running little chick games,
all day long! And it was the
greatest fun EVER!

yippeee!

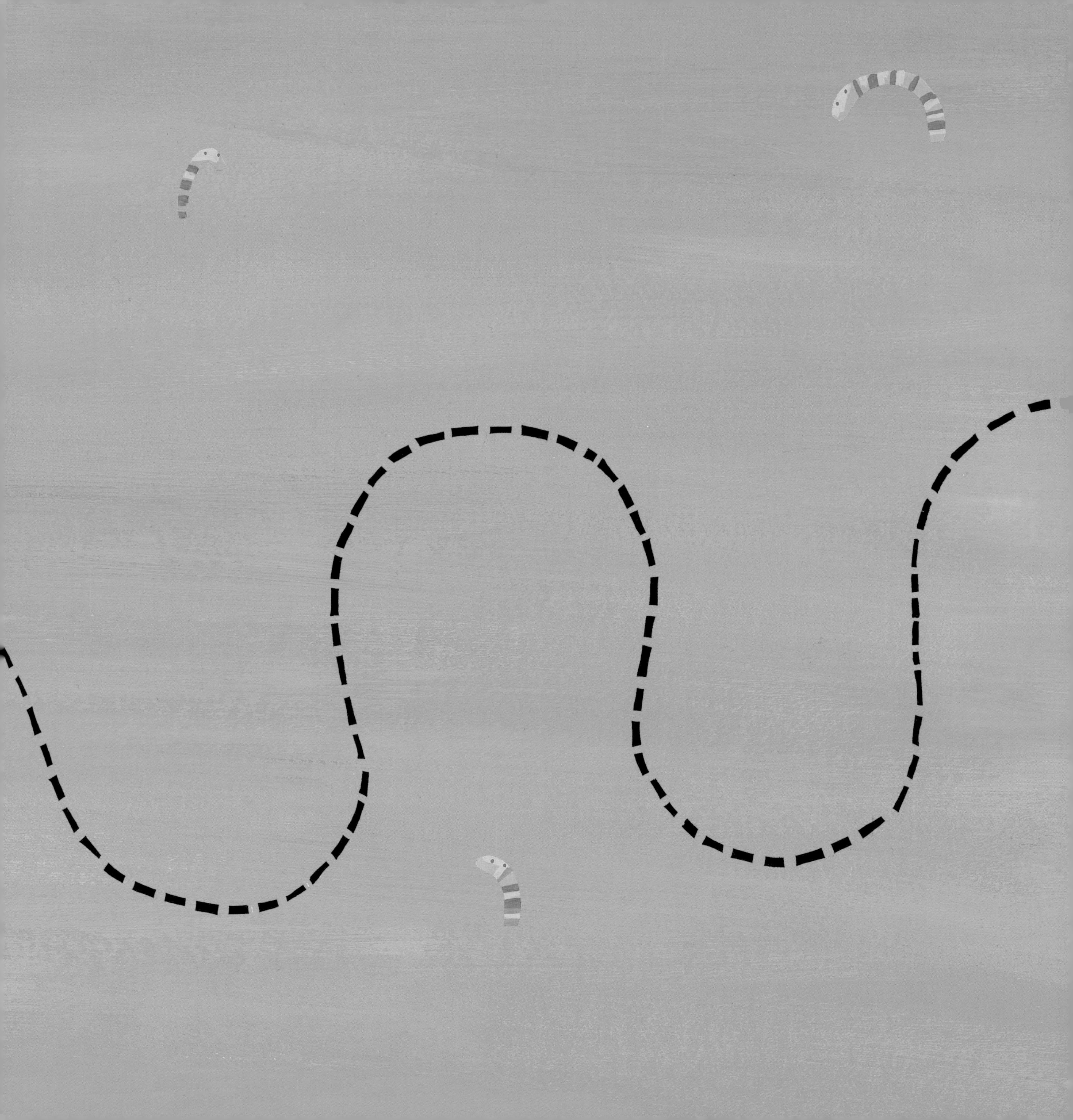

More fabulous books from Little Tiger Press!

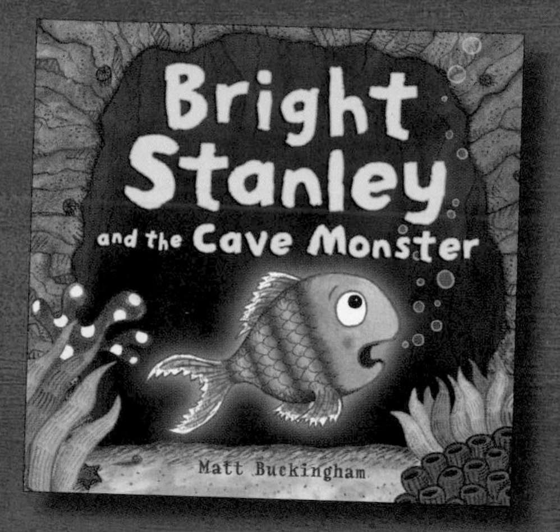

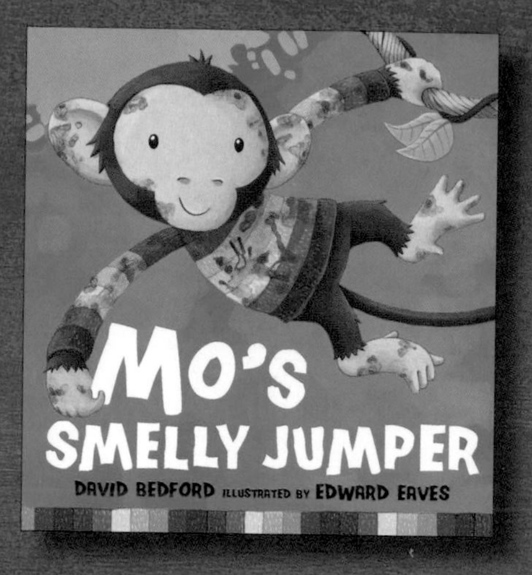

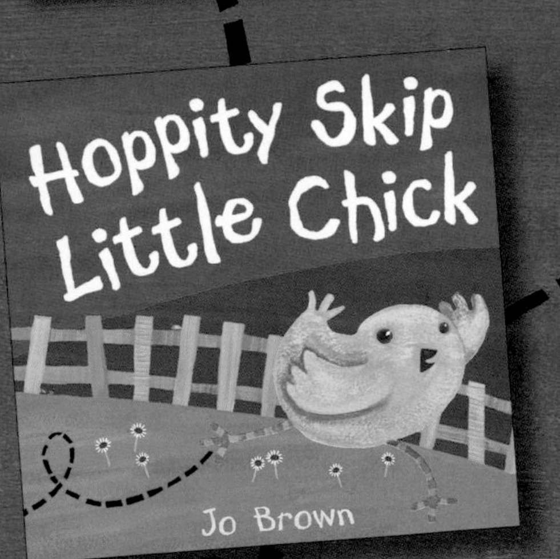

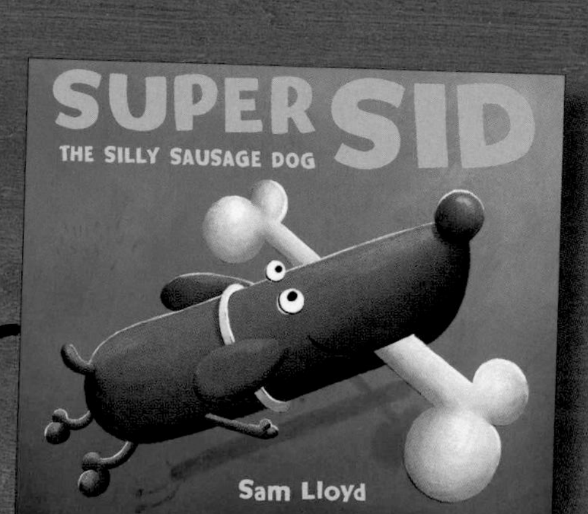

For information regarding any of the above titles
or for our catalogue, please contact us:
Little Tiger Press, 1 The Coda Centre,
189 Munster Road, London SW6 6AW
Tel: 020 7385 6333 • E-mail: contact@littletiger.co.uk
www.littletiger.co.uk